Put Beginning Readers on the Right Track with
ALL ABOARD READING™

The All Aboard Reading series is especially designed for beginning readers. Written by noted authors and illustrated in full color, these are books that children really want to read—books to excite their imagination, expand their interests, make them laugh, and support their feelings. With fiction and nonfiction stories that are high interest and curriculum-related, All Aboard Reading books offer something for every young reader. And with four different reading levels, the All Aboard Reading series lets you choose which books are most appropriate for your children and their growing abilities.

Picture Readers
Picture Readers have super-simple texts, with many nouns appearing as rebus pictures. At the end of each book are 24 flash cards—on one side is a rebus picture; on the other side is the written-out word.

Station Stop 1
Station Stop 1 books are best for children who have just begun to read. Simple words and big type make these early reading experiences more comfortable. Picture clues help children to figure out the words on the page. Lots of repetition throughout the text helps children to predict the next word or phrase—an essential step in developing word recognition.

Station Stop 2
Station Stop 2 books are written specifically for children who are reading with help. Short sentences make it easier for early readers to understand what they are reading. Simple plots and simple dialogue help children with reading comprehension.

Station Stop 3
Station Stop 3 books are perfect for children who are reading alone. With longer text and harder words, these books appeal to children who have mastered basic reading skills. More complex stories captivate children who are ready for more challenging books.

In addition to All Aboard Reading books, look for All Aboard Math Readers™ (fiction stories that teach math concepts children are learning in school) and All Aboard Science Readers™ (nonfiction books that explore the most fascinating science topics in age-appropriate language).

All Aboard for happy reading!

To Genevieve—J.B.S.

For Yvonne and her three dogs—C.D.

Text copyright © 2002 by Judith Bauer Stamper. Illustrations copyright © 2002 by Chris Demarest. All rights reserved. Published by Grosset & Dunlap, a division of Penguin Putnam Books for Young Readers, 345 Hudson Street, New York, NY 10014. GROSSET & DUNLAP and ALL ABOARD MATH READER are trademarks of Penguin Putnam Inc. Published simultaneously in Canada. Printed in the U.S.A.

Library of Congress Cataloging-in-Publication Data is available.

ISBN 0-448-42845-8 (pbk)   C D E F G H I J
ISBN 0-448-42874-1 (GB)   A B C D E F G H I J

THE BOWWOW BAKE SALE

By Judith Bauer Stamper
Illustrated by Chris Demarest

Grosset & Dunlap • New York

Chapter 1
A Puppy Named Penny

School was out for the day. Sam, Tim, Gwen, and Emily were walking home together. They all lived in the same apartment building.

"I'm hungry," Sam said.

"Me, too!" Gwen added.

"Let's stop at Dino's Deli," Tim said. "We can buy a snack."

"Maybe if we add up all our money together, we'll have enough to buy something <u>really</u> good," Emily said.

Sam reached into his pocket. "I have 45¢."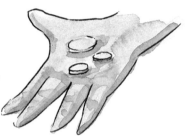

 "I found a quarter and a nickel," said Tim.

Gwen pulled open her backpack. "Here are two quarters."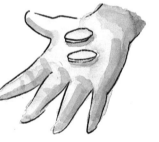

 "And I have two dimes and a nickel," Emily said. She pulled out a notepad and pencil. She added up all the money.

"Our grand total is one dollar and fifty cents!" Emily exclaimed. "Let's see what we can buy."

The friends stopped in front of Dino's Deli. Tim was the first to see the sign in the window.

"I have always wanted a puppy," Tim said. "But my mom says that puppies cost a lot of money."

"We can ask Dino about it," Sam suggested. "But first, let's buy something to eat. I'm starving."

The friends walked into Dino's Deli. They headed for the snacks. They looked at all the prices.

Puppy needs home.
Ask Dino

"Check out these animal crackers," Sam said. "It's a big box. And they only cost $1.49."

"Sold!" Emily said. She picked up the box and headed to the front of the store.

"I want an elephant," Sam said

"I want a hippo," Emily added.

"I want a lion," Gwen said.

"Does anybody want a dog?" Dino asked as they came up to the counter. Then he sneezed.

"*Achoo!*"

The sneeze was followed by a loud bark. "*Woof*!"

A puppy with golden fur jumped out from behind the counter. She ran to Gwen and begged for attention.

Gwen bent down to pet the puppy. "Is this the puppy that needs a home?" she asked.

"I just got her," said Dino. "But I can't keep her. I'm allergic . . . *achoo*!"

"*Woof*!" barked the puppy. She jumped up on Emily. She tried to get the string handle of the animal cracker box with her paw.

"What's her name?" Sam asked, laughing.

"I call her Penny," Dino explained. He reached into his cash register and pulled out a penny. "She's the same color as a bright new penny."

Emily put the box of animal crackers on the counter. She laid down $1.50 in coins.

"That's exactly the change we need," she said, picking up the penny.

"But where will Penny go if you can't keep her?" Gwen asked.

"I don't know. That's the problem," Dino said. "Penny needs a new home . . . *achoo*!"

"*Woof*!" Penny barked. She panted happily.

"It would be so much fun to have a dog," Gwen said, petting Penny. "We could walk her after school."

"Would you like to take Penny for a
walk now?" Dino asked. "I'll pay you
a dollar for the job."

"Sure!" the kids yelled together.

"Could we take Penny home and show
her to my mom?" Tim asked. "I've always
wanted a dog, and when she sees Penny,
I know she'll want one, too!"

"That would be great," Dino said. "But remember, having a puppy can cost a lot of money."

"But Penny would be worth every cent!" Tim said.

"No, Penny!" Emily suddenly yelled. "Give it back!"

Everyone looked at Penny. The box of animal crackers dangled from her mouth.

Tim grabbed for the box. But Penny jumped away. Sam sneaked up from behind. But Penny ran through his legs. Finally, Gwen caught Penny. She pulled the box from the puppy's mouth.

"Sit, Penny," Gwen ordered.

"*Woof*!" Penny barked. Then she jumped up again for the box.

"Penny!" everyone yelled.

Chapter Two
Penny, Nickels, and Dimes

As soon as the kids brought Penny to Tim's house, they fed her the dog food that Dino had sent along.

"Oh, no, she's eaten a whole bowl of food already!" Gwen said.

Penny ate up the last pieces of dog food. Then she looked up at everyone and panted happily.

Tim's mom came in with a bowl full of water.

"This dog will eat us out of house and home," she said. Then she smiled and petted Penny's head.

"Can we keep her, Mom?" Tim asked. "Please?"

"Please, Mrs. Smith!" all the kids said.

Mrs. Smith picked up Penny in her arms.

"She is very cute. But having a puppy is a lot of hard work, and it's also very expensive," said Tim's mom.

"We will all pitch in to pay for her food!" the kids told her.

"If you can help buy her food, and if you can help raise money for everything else she needs . . . then I think Penny has a new home."

Penny reached up and licked Mrs. Smith's face.

"*Woof*!" she barked.

Emily took out her notebook and pencil.

"We need a plan," she said. She led everyone into the living room. "First, let's figure out the cost of food."

"Dino told me he would sell us dog food at a discount," Gwen said. "He thought it would be about $12.00 a month."

"Okay," Emily said, writing in her notebook. "$12.00 a month divided by four is $3.00 each a month."

"I get $2.00 a week allowance," Sam said. "If I save 75¢ a week, that would equal $3.00 a month."

"My mom said I could earn extra money recycling bottles and cans," Gwen said. "So put me down for $3.00 a month."

"Put me down for the money, too," Tim said. "Maybe Dino can give me a little job every week. Then I can earn enough money to help pay for the food."

"I'm in for $3.00 too," Emily said. "Did you hear that, Penny? We have a plan to feed you!"

"Speaking of food, I'm still hungry," Sam said. "Where are the animal crackers?"

Emily pulled the box of animal crackers out of her backpack. She passed them around.

"Penny still needs a lot of puppy stuff," Gwen said.

"Like a flea collar," Tim said. He scratched his leg.

"And a doggy bowl," Mrs. Smith called out from the kitchen.

"And a new leash," Sam said. "Plus she will have to go to the vet for a checkup."

Emily busily added up numbers in her notebook.

"I think we need to raise $50," she said, "just to be safe."

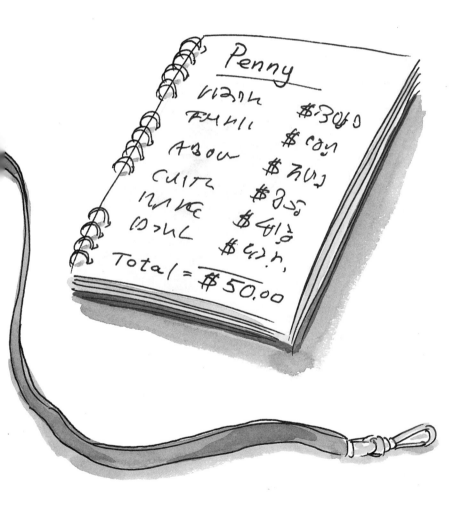

"Penny!" Gwen yelled. "That's my animal cracker!"

Penny licked her mouth. "*Woof*!" she barked.

"Wait a minute," Emily said. "I know how we can raise money for Penny's supplies! We can sell homemade doggy treats."

"Cool!" Sam said. "But how? We don't know how to make doggy treats!"

"I'll be right back!" Emily said. "I saw a recipe in one of my mom's magazines."

Emily ran upstairs to her apartment.
In a few minutes she was back. She gave
Sam the magazine.

"Lucky Dog Doggy Treats," Sam said.
"Look, they are even shaped like bones!"
"*Woof*!" Penny barked.

"We can make the treats tomorrow after school," Gwen said, "and sell them in the park on Saturday!"

"We can call it the Bowwow Bake Sale!" Emily said.

"How many treats will we have to sell to make $50?" Tim asked.

"Let's see, if we sell each treat for a quarter, that would be four treats for a dollar," Emily said.

"So to earn $50, we have to sell 200 doggy treats," Sam said.

"But we need to buy the ingredients first," Emily said. "Go get your spare change, everybody."

Twenty minutes later, everyone was back with a pile of coins.

"Let's put the coins in piles that equal a dollar," Tim said.

"The quarters go in stacks of four,"
Gwen said.

"Ten dimes equal a dollar," Emily said.

"Twenty nickels make a dollar,"
Sam said.

"And a hundred pennies make a
dollar!" Tim said.

When all the coins were put in stacks,
Emily added them up.

12 Quarters = $ 3.00
18 Dimes = $ 1.80
52 Nickels = $ 2.60
90 Pennies = $ .90
_____
$ 8.30

Total

"Perfect! We have $8.30 to buy the flour, the cookie cutter, and everything else we need," Emily said.

Just then, Penny ran toward the coins. She sat down in the middle of the money and wagged her tail.

"Penny!" everyone screamed.

Chapter Three
The Bowwow Bake Sale

"Everything is ready!" Emily said.

Sam, Gwen, Tim, and Emily stood behind the table. The doggy bones were in neat piles. The kids had worked very hard to make them. A sign was hung on a tree beside the table. Penny sat in front. She wore a red bandanna with her name on it.

"Here comes our first customer!" Gwen said.

A woman walked up with a big sheepdog. The dog sniffed Penny. The woman looked at the treats.

"Are these homemade?" she asked.

"We made them ourselves," Gwen said. "We're raising money to adopt Penny."

"My dog will try one treat," the woman said. She handed Emily one quarter.

DELICIOUS DOGGY TREATS
1 Bone   25¢
4 Bones $1.00

Emily took the money and put it in the cash box. Sam handed the woman a bone. The sheepdog jumped up and ate the bone in one bite.

"*Woof*!" it barked. Then it licked its
mouth.

"I think I'll buy four more!" The woman said and laughed. She gave another dollar to Emily.

"5 bones sold, 195 to go!" Tim said.

Soon, business was booming at the Bowwow Bake Sale.

"I'll take 8 bones for my boxer,"
a man said.

"Two dollars, please," Emily said.

"Here is a dollar," a woman with a
collie said. "I want three bones."

"A quarter is your change," Gwen said.

"It's my dog's birthday today," a man said. "He's ten years old. I'll take ten treats."

"That will be . . . $2.50," Tim said.

"I only have a five-dollar bill," the man said.

"Don't worry, we have plenty of change," Emily said. She opened the cash box. "Here is $2.50 back."

A girl walked up with a beagle.

"These cookies are so cute!" she said. "I want to buy some for Buster."

The girl reached into her pocket. She pulled out 5 dimes. "How many can I get for this?" she asked.

"5 dimes equals 50¢," Sam said. "You can buy 2 bones."

At noon, Tim's mother brought everyone peanut butter sandwiches. She looked at the table. Almost all the bones were gone.

"How many bones did you sell?" she asked.

Emily did a quick count. "There are only 15 bones left! That means we sold 185!"

$$\begin{array}{r} 200 \\ -185 \\ \hline 15 \end{array}$$

Just then, a man with a dalmatian stopped by.

"I'll take a dozen treats," he said. "This is great! I've never been to a Bowwow Bake Sale before."

"A dozen is 12," Emily explained.

Tim counted out 12 bones and put them in a big bag. Emily put the man's three dollars into the cash box.

"Count the money, Emily," Sam said.
"How much do we have?"
Emily counted the bills first.

29 $1 bills = $29.00

1 $5 bill = $5.00

Then she counted the coins.

48 quarters = $12.00

20 dimes   = $2.00

25 nickels   = $1.25

"The total is $49.25!"

"Only 75¢ to go, Mom," Tim said. "All we have to do is sell the last three doggy treats."

Everyone looked down at the table. The three bones had disappeared!

"Penny!" everyone yelled.

Penny licked her mouth. She smiled at everyone and panted.

Mrs. Smith opened her purse. She pulled out three quarters.

"I'd like to buy three doggy treats for my dog," she said with a smile.

Emily put the quarters in the cash box.

"That makes a grand total of $50.00!" she said. "And Penny has a new home."

Everyone started to cheer.
"*Woof*!" barked Penny.